CW00847254

THE WAY TO TREASURE ISLAND

For curious Dads everywhere (especially mine),
and the daughters who put up with them - L.S.

Inspiring | Educating | Creating | Entertaining

Brimming with creative inspiration, how-to projects, and useful
information to enrich your everyday life, Quarto Knows is a favourite
destination for those pursuing their interests and passions. Visit our
site and dig deeper with our books into your area of interest:
Quarto Creates, Quarto Cooks, Quarto Homes, Quarto Lives,
Quarto Drives, Quarto Explores, Quarto Gifts, or Quarto Kids.

Text and illustrations © Lizzy Stewart 2019.
First published in 2019 by Frances Lincoln Children's Books.
First published in paperback in 2020 by Frances Lincoln Children's Books,
an imprint of the Quarto Group.
The Old Brewery, 6 Blundell Street, London N7 9BH, United Kingdom.
T (0)20 7700 6700 F (0)20 7700 8066 www.QuartoKnows.com
The right of Lizzy Stewart to be identified as the author and illustrator of this work
has been asserted by her in accordance with the Copyright, Designs and Patents Act,
1988 (United Kingdom).
All rights reserved.
No part of this publication may be reproduced, stored in a retrieval system, or transmitted,
in any form, or by any means, electrical, mechanical, photocopying, recording or otherwise without
the prior written permission of the publisher or a licence permitting restricted copying.
A catalogue record for this book is available from the British Library.
ISBN 978-0-7112-4392-7
The illustrations were created with pencil and watercolour
Set in Old Claude
Published by Rachel Williams
Designed by Zoë Tucker
Edited by Katie Cotton
Production by Caragh McAleenan
Manufactured in Guangdong, China CC 012020
1 3 5 7 9 8 6 4 2

LIZZY STEWART

THE WAY TO TREASURE ISLAND

Frances Lincoln
Children's Books

This is Matilda,

and this is
Matilda's dad.

They're the best of friends, but they don't always
see eye to eye. In fact, they're total opposites!

Fast and slow.

Tidy and
messy.

Quiet and very,
very noisy.

Matilda and her dad
are very different,
but they always
have fun together.

Well, nearly always.

One day, Matilda and Dad are at the beach. Matilda
has a special map. She's going to find treasure!
"Can I come too?" asks Dad.

"Okay…" says Matilda. "But we have to follow this map. It's very important. The treasure's right there, where the big, red X is. So no getting distracted!"

"I **never** get distracted," says Dad.

Matilda and her dad find
an old wooden boat and set sail.

Through her telescope, Matilda can see the
far-away island. "Dad, we need to go left
then right then left," she says.

Dad doesn't reply.
"You're looking the wrong
way, Dad," Matilda sighs.

"Looking the wrong way?" says Matilda's
Dad. "I'm not. Look down. It's…"

"Incredible!" says Matilda.

"We better get going though," she adds, after a while. "We've got to find the treasure."

But by the time Dad has finished,
they've floated far out to sea.
"Let's take a short-cut," says Dad.
"There's NO shortcut on the map,"
says Matilda...

but it's too late.

"Round here,"
says Dad.

"Through
here..."

"Look at that!"

"Dad, now we're lost!" says Matilda.
"Lost?" says Dad. "Of course we're not lost."
"We just need to go back round this nice, big rock…"

The giant wave carries Matilda and Dad
to the shore of the treasure island!

"That's lucky!" laughs Dad,
picking seaweed from his hair.
"Let's try not to get lost again," says
Matilda crossly, looking at her map.

Once they're off the boat, Matilda points to a path towards the mountains. "It's this way," she says.

"That way?" says Dad. "But this way looks much more fun."

"The map says it's this way," says Matilda.
"So I'm going this way!"

"I tell you what," says Dad.
"You go that way and I'll go
this way. We'll see who finds
the treasure first!"

"Fine," says Matilda.

So Matilda and Dad set off
in different directions.

Dad gets distracted by all sorts
of exciting things.

But without Matilda there to lead the way, soon he's completely and utterly lost.

Matilda follows the map
really, really closely.

She's sure she's going the right way, but without
her dad to show her all the exciting things he sees, it's a
bit boring. Finally, Matilda finds the place on the map
where the treasure should be.

She looks everywhere.

Under things,

over things,

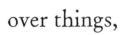

and even
inside things.

"I don't understand," says Matilda.
"The treasure should be right here, but it isn't!"

"Maybe Dad found it without me," Matilda says sadly. "I should go back to the boat before he wonders where I am." She looks at the map. "It must be this way."

"Matilda will be waiting for me,"
says Dad. "I bet she found the treasure
aaaaages ago." He looks around.
"I wonder what's in here…"

"Treasure!"